# The CAT and the MOUSE

AN ENGLISH
FOLKTALE RETOLD BY

## Edel Wignell

ILLUSTRATED BY

## Mini Goss

HOUGHTON MIFFLIN COMPANY

BOSTON

ATLANTA   DALLAS   GENEVA, ILLINOIS   PALO ALTO   PRINCETON

Once upon a time, a cat and
a mouse were playing in a barn.
The cat bit off the mouse's tail.

"Ooh, give me back my tail!" squealed the mouse.

"No," said the cat. "First, you must go to the cow and get me some milk. Then I will give you back your tail."

The mouse went to the cow. "Please cow, will you give me some milk for the cat? Then the cat will give me back my tail."

"No," said the cow. "First, you must go to the farmer and get me some hay."

The mouse went to the farmer. "Please farmer, will you give me some hay for the cow? Then the cow will give me milk for the cat, and the cat will give me back my tail."

"No," said the farmer. "First, you must go to the butcher and get me some meat."

The mouse went to the butcher. "Please butcher, will you give me some meat for the farmer? Then the farmer will give me some hay for the cow. The cow will give me some milk for the cat, and the cat will give me back my tail."

"No," said the butcher. "First, you must go to the baker and get me some bread."

The mouse went to the baker.

"Please baker, will you give me some bread for the butcher? Then the butcher will give me some meat for the farmer. The farmer will give me some hay for the cow. The cow will give me some milk for the cat, and the cat will give me back my tail."

"Yes," said the baker. "But you must promise not to eat my flour."

The mouse promised, "I will not eat your flour."

Then the baker gave bread for the butcher, the butcher gave meat for the farmer, the farmer gave hay for the cow, and the cow gave milk for the cat.

And, at long last, the cat gave back the mouse's tail.